For Mike and Cara, with love

Published in Great Britain by
Inside Pocket Publishing Limited

First published in Great Britain in 2011
Text © Felix Arthur, 2010

The right of Felix Arthur to be identified
as the author of this work has been asserted
in accordance with the
Copyright, Designs and Patents Act 1988

Illustrations © Jenny Capon 2011

A CIP catalogue record for this book is available from
the British Library

ISBN 978-0-9567122-3-3

Inside Pocket Publishing Limited Reg. No. 06580097

Printed and bound in Great Britain by
Ashford Colour Press

www.insidepocket.co.uk

The Golden Prince

by Felix Arthur

Illustrated by Jenny Capon

Once upon a time
there was a
Brave Knight
known as the
Golden Prince.

He lived in
a Big Castle
at the top of
a Very High
Mountain.

He was always
rescuing
Damsels in
Distress...

Hunting
Wild Beasts
in the Forest...

And locking up
Traitors
in the Dungeon!

His Father, the King,
was often busy with
Affairs of State.

His Mother, the Queen,
spent much of her time
making sure the Castle
ran smoothly.

One Day, the Castle
was attacked by a
Fierce Dragon and a
Mighty Wizard!

The Golden Prince
fought bravely and
defeated them both.

A Great Feast was
held in Celebration.

Afterwards, the Queen washed the Brave Knight from Head to Toe...

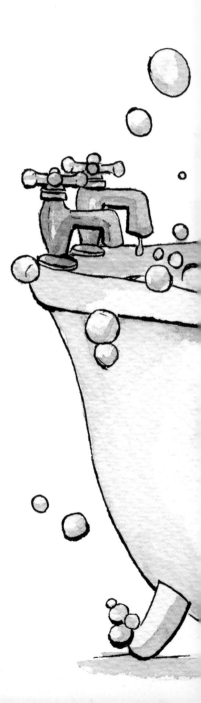

And put him to bed
with a Magical Kiss.

Cat

Helmet

Sword

Shield

Duck

Cloak

Also by Felix Arthur and Jenny Capon